GOOD NIGHT, LITTLE BEAR

BY PATSY SCARRY
PICTURES BY RICHARD SCARRY

🅖 A GOLDEN BOOK • NEW YORK

Copyright © 1961, renewed 1989 by Random House, Inc. All rights reserved under International and Pan-American Copyright Conventions. Published in the United States by Golden Books, an imprint of Random House Children's Books, a division of Random House, Inc., New York, and simultaneously in Canada by Random House of Canada Limited, Toronto. Originally published in 1961 by Golden Press, Inc. Golden Books, A Golden Book, A Little Golden Book, the G colophon, and the distinctive gold spine are registered trademarks of Random House, Inc. A Little Golden Book Classic is a trademark of Random House, Inc. Library of Congress Control Number: 00-109704
ISBN: 0-307-98624-1
www.goldenbooks.com
Printed in the United States of America   First Random House Edition 2002

10

It is time for Little Bear to go to bed.
Mother Bear closes the storybook.
She gives Little Bear a good-night kiss.

Then over to
his big furry father
runs the little bear.

Wheee!

Father Bear swings his little one high up
to his shoulders for a ride to bed.

"Duck your head," calls Mother Bear, just in time.
And into the snug little bedroom they go.

Squeak!

The tiny bed sighs as Father Bear sits down.

"Now, into bed with you," he says.

He waits for Little Bear to climb down.

But Little Bear doesn't move.

He sits up on his father's shoulders and grins.

Father Bear waits. He yawns a rumbly yawn.

Is Father Bear falling asleep?

No. Suddenly he opens his eyes again.

"Why, I must have been dreaming,"
says Father Bear, pretending to wake up.
But what's this?
There is no furry head on the pillow.
Where can Little Bear be?
Father Bear looks under the pillow.
Nobody there.
He doesn't seem to feel
something tickling his ear.

Aha.
There's a lump down under the blanket.
Father Bear pats the lump.
But it doesn't squeak or wiggle.
Can it be Little Bear?

Why, it's the toy teddy and the blue bunny
waiting for Little Bear to come to bed!

"Mother, that naughty bear is hiding,"
says Father Bear to Mother Bear, with a wink.
"Maybe he's hiding under the kitchen stove,"
says Mother Bear, who loves a joke.

Bang! Bang!
Father Bear rattles the pots and pans
on top of the stove.
"Little Bear, I'm coming to get you!" he roars.

Father Bear reaches under the stove.
He feels something soft and furry.
Is it Little Bear?

No.
It's only Father Bear's old winter mitten.

'Way up high Little Bear claps his paw
to his mouth. But not in time.
"I heard that Little Bear laugh," says Father.
"Now where can he be hiding?

"Is he standing outside the front door?
I'll turn the knob softly —
and fling the door wide!"
No. There are no bears out there.
Just a family of fat little rabbits
nibbling lettuce in the garden.
"Shoo!" snorts Father Bear.

"Something is hiding in the woodbox,"
whispers Mother Bear.
"Creep over there on tip toe,
and you may catch a little bear."
Eeek!
There's just a wee mouse hiding there.

There's nobody up high, on the china shelf.
"Ouch!"
Little Bear bumps his head.
"Who said Ouch?" asks Father Bear.
"Mother, did you say Ouch?"
"Not I," smiles Mother Bear.
Oh she is a tease.

"Now where is that naughty bear hiding?
He wouldn't run away.
Not a little bear who is always hungry
for chocolate cake."
And that big Daddy Bear cuts himself a huge piece
of chocolate cake right under the little bear's nose.

Little Bear suddenly feels hungry.
But just then Father Bear stops smack
in front of the mirror.
"Why, there he is," roars the big bear.
"But you couldn't find me," squeaks Little Bear,
reaching for chocolate cake.

Wheee!
Off Daddy's shoulders and down to the sofa.
Bounce. Bounce. Bounce.
"Wasn't that a good hiding place, Mommy?
No one could find me up there."

"But I've found you now," says Father Bear.
Little Bear wiggles and giggles under his Daddy's
strong arm . . . all the way into bed.

"Did I really fool you, Daddy?"
asks Little Bear.
Father Bear just laughs and winks.
Do you think Father Bear knew all the time?